Cool as a Cucumber

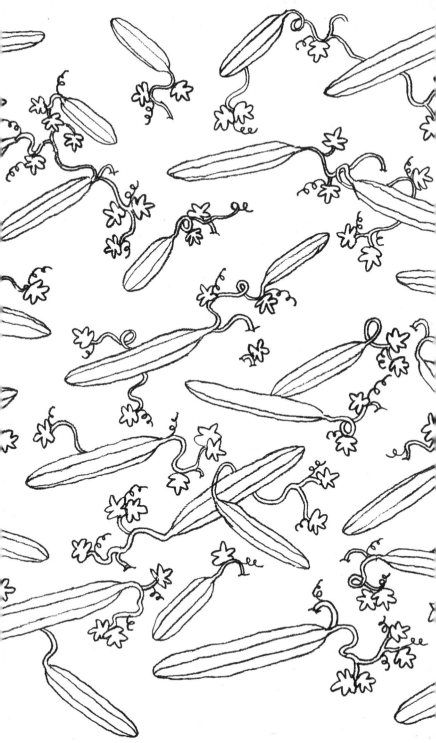

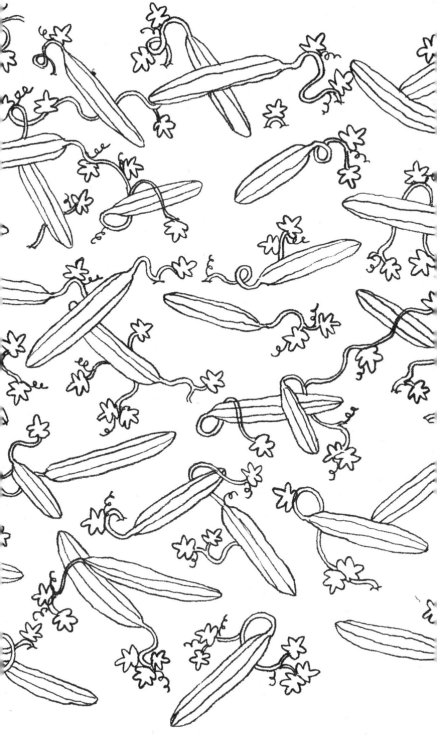

Other books by Michael Morpurgo:

Cool as a Cucumber

Michael Morpurgo
Illustrated by Tor Freeman

WALKER
BOOKS

For Esther

First published 2003 by Walker Books Ltd
87 Vauxhall Walk, London SE11 5HJ

This edition published 2017

2 4 6 8 10 9 7 5 3 1

Text © 2003 Michael Morpurgo
Illustrations © 2003 Tor Freeman

The right of Michael Morpurgo and Tor Freeman to be identified as author
and illustrator respectively of this work has been asserted by them
in accordance with the Copyright, Designs and Patents Act 1988

This book has been typeset in Garamond

Printed in Great Britain by Clays Ltd, St Ives plc

British Library Cataloguing in Publication Data:
a catalogue record for this book is available from the British Library

ISBN 978-1-4063-7872-6

www.walker.co.uk

Contents

Chapter One

Last summer I was a hero. Not for long. Just long enough to grow a giant cucumber, a cucumber fit for a queen.

The whole thing began one morning when Mrs Mapleton came into class all bright-eyed and bubbly with excitement.

"I had the most brilliant idea last night, children," she said. "In the bath." She's always having brilliant ideas in her bath.

"I've been wracking my brain for weeks to find something we could all do to celebrate the Queen's Jubilee. Guess what? We're going to dig our very own school vegetable garden! We'll call it the Queen's Jubilee Garden.

We're going to grow our own
vegetables, children – carrots,
potatoes, onions, parsley."

What's parsley, miss?

"What's parsley, miss?" asked
Mandy Sharp, who loves asking
questions.

Mrs Mapleton ignored her. "And
cucumbers," she went on. "We're
going to grow cucumbers too.

Maybe we'll send one to the
Queen so that she can make lots of
cucumber sandwiches. Well, what
do you think of that, children?"

To be honest, none of us was that
keen at first. I think it was the word
"dig" that worried us. But Mrs
Mapleton had enough enthusiasm
for all of us, and very soon we were
all really looking forward to it.

So there we were that same afternoon digging over the patch of wasteland between the playing fields and the hedge, Mrs Mapleton urging us on.

"The sooner we get this done," she told us, "the sooner we can get the horse manure dug in – horse manure's by far the best for vegetables, children.

Then we can get our seeds
planted out, and before you know
it – *licketysplit* – we'll have our first
vegetables. The first cucumber
goes to the hardest worker."

I like cucumbers, so I dug a little harder. I soon discovered that digging was a lot more fun than I'd ever imagined it could be, because I began finding all sorts of really interesting things.

The longest, fattest, wriggliest worm I had ever seen,

a tomato sauce bottle,

a giant beetle with nasty evil-looking pincers,

bits and pieces of blue and white china

and even a shoe –

well, a sort of sandal with one strap and a rusty buckle.

18

Every time I found something, I'd run over to show it to Mrs Mapleton. But I soon discovered that she wasn't nearly as interested in my treasures as I thought she'd be. I asked her if my sandal might be a Roman one, if my blue and white china was from Tudor times – we'd just been doing the Tudors.

"Who knows, Peter? Maybe you could make up one of your lovely stories about it. You're such a dreamer," she laughed. "But now is not the time for dreaming. Now is the time for digging. We're trying to grow a cucumber for the Queen, remember? Back to your digging now, there's a good boy."

Chapter Two

So off I went back to my digging.
But I kept finding more and more
things in the earth, exciting things
that I wanted to keep. I decided
not to show Mrs Mapleton any
more of my new treasures.

Instead I made a secret pile of them
in the long grass by the hedge.

I was looking for coins now.
For gold maybe! I dug and I dug
and I dug.

By the time the bell rang for playtime I was having such a good time that I asked Mrs Mapleton if I could stay behind and go on with my digging. Mrs Mapleton seemed a bit surprised. "Of course, Peter," she said. "But don't you go digging up any old tombs or pirate's treasure while I'm gone, will you?" And away she went across the playground, her laughter tinkling in the air.

Once she'd gone, I used her fork. It was bigger than mine, so I could dig deeper with it. In no time at all I had found the other sandal – with the strap missing – and best of all a one penny coin, with a date on it: 1901. Over a hundred years old!

But by now I was getting tired. My hand was hurting – I had a huge blister coming up. One last try, I thought. Could be gold this time, you never know.

I plunged my fork in again and stamped on it as hard as I could. But it just wouldn't go in, no matter how hard I stamped. I thought I must have hit a stone or a rock or something. I got down on my knees and scraped away the earth with my bare hands.

Whatever it was, it was very big
and very round, and very long.
And it wasn't stone or rock. It was
metal. The more I dug, the bigger
and rounder and longer it seemed
to get.

At last, after several minutes of hard digging, I found where it ended. It was massive – five of my steps long, and with a point at one end. The other end was still buried. It looked like a giant black cucumber. I wondered if there was a point at the other end too.

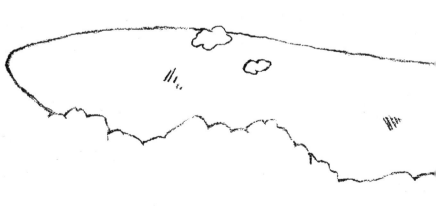

But instead of a point I discovered
a sort of fin. That was when I began
to realize what it was. A bomb! It
was a huge black bomb!

I dropped the fork and backed away. I'd been digging round a bomb! It could go off at any moment. Fear crept up my back like a cold hand. I turned and ran.

Chapter Three

I hared across the playing field, crashed open the school door and made for the staffroom. I burst in.

Mrs Mapleton was standing by the notice-board drinking her tea. All the other teachers just gaped.

None of them looked at all pleased to see me, not even Mrs Mapleton.

"Peter!" said Mrs Mapleton. "This is the staffroom. You know you should knock."

"It's a bomb, miss! In the Queen's Jubilee Garden, miss. I've dug up a bomb!"

For just a moment there was silence. Then one of the teachers laughed. "You sure it's not a giant cucumber, Peter?" They didn't believe me. Now they were all laughing, except Mrs Mapleton, who came over to me and put her arm round me gently.

"Peter's my very best digger," she said. "He may have a rather vivid imagination sometimes, but there's nothing wrong with that. He's going to be a writer when he grows up, aren't you, Peter? Off you go now, dear. I'll be out when I've finished my tea."

"But miss, it's a bomb, a real bomb. Honest!"

Mrs Mapleton sighed. "All right Peter. I'll come in a minute." And she waved me away. "Go on, out you go. I won't be long. Out. *Out.*"

Out!

She didn't believe me either. I could hear in her voice that she didn't believe me.

So I did just what she'd told me. I went out. I went *right* out. I went out of the school gates, past the church, down the road to the phone box, where I dialled 999.

"Which service do you require? Fire? Ambulance? Police?" said the voice.

"All of them," I replied. "I've found a bomb in my school, while I was digging in the Queen's Jubilee Garden. It's big, very big."

"And what school is that?"

"St Peter's. Past the church."

"And what's your name?"

"Peter."

"Someone'll be right there, Peter," said the voice.

After that everything seemed to happen very fast. Only minutes later, just as playtime was ending, the fire engines came – four of them –

then three police cars and two ambulances – lights flashing, sirens whooping and whining. All the teachers came running out.

Everyone just stood in the playground and gawped. Except me.

One of the policemen called out, "Where's the bomb then?"

"Over there," I told him, pointing across the playing field to the Queen's Jubilee Garden.

"By the hedge," I said.

They went and had a look. One look was enough. The playground was cleared. The school was cleared. The traffic was stopped. No trains ran. The whole world went silent and waited.

By now everyone – the police, the firefighters, the paramedics, all my friends, Mum, Dad; everyone, including the teachers and Mrs Mapleton – all of them were saying how wonderful, how brave I had been. I glowed inside and felt very heroic and important. I liked that feeling, I liked it a lot.

Chapter Four

About teatime there was a big bang
and everything shook. Then we
were allowed to go home. I saw all
about it on the TV news that
evening – after my press conference
that is, after all the interviews with
the TV people and the newspapers
in our front garden.

"A controlled explosion" they called it on the news.

Apparently it was an old bomb from the war, one that had fallen on the town sixty years before without exploding.

I saw *me* on the news too, with Mrs Mapleton beside me saying how proud she was of me, and how when I'd discovered the bomb I'd done just the right thing.

Mum and Dad said they were proud of me too – which they'd never said before. Still, I suppose I'd never discovered a bomb before, had I?

"What was it like to find a bomb in your school garden?" one reporter asked, practically shoving his microphone down my throat.

And, cool as a cucumber, I said, "Cool. Really cool."

I was front page news in all the papers the next morning. Mum bought every copy of every paper she could find. PETER SAVES ST PETER'S was one headline. But the one I liked best was PETER'S GIANT CUCUMBER.

That summer, after we'd filled in the crater left by the bomb, we grew lots and lots of vegetables in our Queen's Jubilee Garden. We were all very proud of it – Mrs Mapleton most of all.

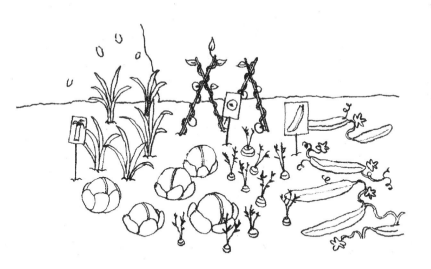

The cucumbers were huge too —
because of all the horse manure
we'd dug in, Mrs Mapleton said.
And I got to take the first
cucumber home. "The first one is
for Peter, our hero and our best
digger," Mrs Mapleton said.

Chapter Five

But that was the last time I was
treated like a hero. Pity really.

The next day Mrs Mapleton
broke the exciting news about her
"special trip", and after that
everyone seemed to forget about
me and my bomb. It was another
idea she'd had in the bath.

"Because all you children have worked so hard on the Queen's Jubilee Garden," she said, "I thought we could miss school for a day and go on a special trip."

"Where to?" asked Mandy Sharp.

"To London of course, Mandy. To Buckingham Palace, where else?" said Mrs Mapleton.

"We're going to fill up a basket with our best vegetables, including our biggest cucumber, and we're going to take it up to the palace and give it to the Queen. Well, what do you think of that, children?"

So that's what we did. We all
signed a beautiful card we'd made,
full of photos of our garden and
telling the Queen all about how
we'd grown everything ourselves.
We even told her about the horse
manure!

Then one morning the whole class got into a coach with Mrs Mapleton, and off we went up to London to see the Queen, to give her our vegetables.

As it turned out it was all a bit disappointing because we never did get to see the Queen. Maybe she saw us. I hope so. She's got hundreds of windows to look out of, so she should have seen us. We waved to her lots, but we couldn't give her our basket of vegetables.

Instead we gave them to a
guardsman on the gate who said
how nice they were and that he'd
make sure the Queen got them.

A week later Mrs Mapleton read out a letter in assembly. It said, "Her Majesty wishes to thank all the children at St Peter's School for their lovely gift of vegetables. She particularly wants them to know how much she has enjoyed making cucumber sandwiches out of St Peter's giant cucumber."

We all gave three cheers for the
Queen, and then one for St Peter's
giant cucumber and one for Mrs
Mapleton, because she had started
the whole idea.

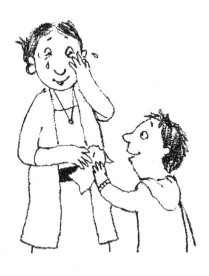

Then Mrs Mapleton cried –
because she was so happy, she said.
Grown-ups do that sometimes.

Funny people grown-ups.

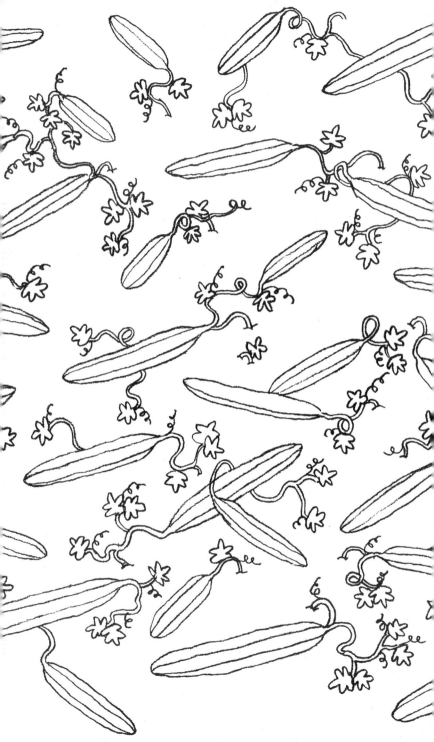

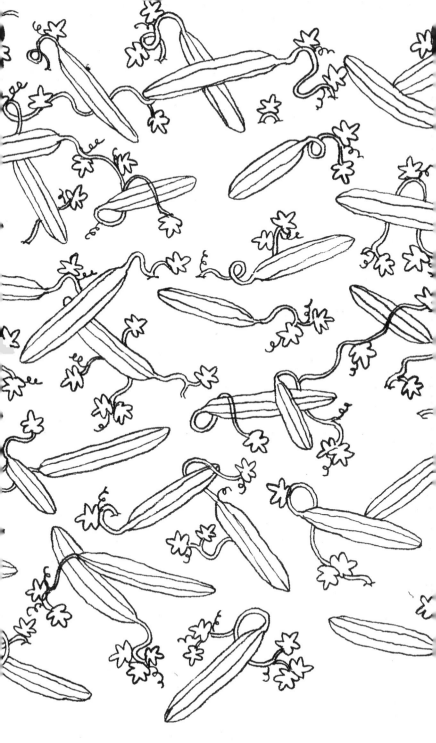

Michael Morpurgo has an unparalleled reputation as a story-maker, is the author of over 100 books and has won numerous major awards for his writing for children. He was also Children's Laureate and has been awarded an OBE for services to literature, and his books are translated and read around the world. Michael and his wife, Clare, founded the charity Farms for City Children and live in Devon.